Do Unto Otters

(A Book About Manners)

For Rilynne

A thank-you song to Christy Ottaviano
to be sung to a tune by The Commodores:

She should change her name to OTTER-viano.

(Chorus)
She's a WORD—HOUSE!
Re-write, re-write me, she takes all my bad words out.
She's a WORD—HOUSE!
Her brain is stacked with lots of facts.
She's nice and she has no plaque.

(Bridge)
She knows nouns, she knows nouns, she knows nouns now. *(Repeat)*

* * *

Thanks, Mom, Scott, and Joan, for your
continuous support and encouragement.

ISBN-13: 978-0-545-10907-9
ISBN-10: 0-545-10907-8

12 11 10 9 8 7 6 5   9 10 11 12 13/0

Printed in the U.S.A.   40

First Scholastic printing, September 2008

The artist used acrylic paint (which she SHARED with her friends) on Arches watercolor paper to CARINGLY create the illustrations for this book. NO TEASING took place during the making of this book. Everyone involved COOPERATED, MADE GOOD EYE CONTACT, and THANKED each other for their hard work. There was one uncomfortable hair-pulling incident that took place toward the end of this project, but everyone involved promptly APOLOGIZED and have since FORGIVEN each other.

This book is based on the Golden Rule.

Otts and ENDS

Hi, Hilde!

Doo-
Dee-
Doo

Do Unto Otters

(A Book About Manners)

By

Laurie Keller

SCHOLASTIC INC.
New York Toronto London Auckland Sydney
Mexico City New Delhi Hong Kong Buenos Aires

EXTRA TWIGS

She could've drawn LESS HEAVY boxes!

ROCKS

THIS END UP

Hello, Mr. Rabbit.
We're your new neighbors,
the OTTERS!

OTTERS?

OTTERS?

My new neighbors are

OTTERS!

I don't know anything about <u>otters</u>.
What if we don't get along?

Mr. Rabbit, I know an old saying:

"DO UNTO OTTERS AS YOU WOULD HAVE OTTERS DO UNTO YOU."

What does **THAT** mean?

It simply means treat otters the same way you'd like otters to treat you.

Treat otters the same way I'd like otters to treat me?

Hmmm...

How would I like otters to treat me?

How would **I** . . .

. . . like **OTTERS** . . .

. . . to treat **ME** ?

Well . . . I'd like otters to be FRIENDLY.

A cheerful hello,

a nice smile,

and good eye contact

are all part of being friendly.

Friendliness is very important to me—especially after my last neighbor, Mrs. Grrrrrr.

I'd like otters to be POLITE.

They should know when to say

"PLEASE"

PLEASE LOOK C:

They should know when to say

"THANK YOU."

THANKS FOR LOOKING! ⊂ :

And they should know when to say

"EXCUSE ME."

EXCUSE ME! BURP

Otters should be

HONEST.

That means they should

KEEP THEIR PROMISES

My word is as good as GOLD (fish)!

NOT LIE

I never lie— it makes my whiskers itch.

NOT CHEAT

Cheating makes my whiskers itch, too. . . . I wonder if I should see a doctor?

I'd like otters to be CONSIDERATE.

You know....

It's always good to have a considerate neighbor.

It wouldn't hurt otters to be KIND.

(Everyone appreciates a kind act
no matter how bad it smells.)

Oh, and what's that word?...

"COOPERATE!"

Otters should learn to cooperate.

Did someone say "OPERATE"?

CO-operate: to work well together

We know how to co-OTTER-ate!

I see otters
like to play.

Wheeeeeee!

I'd like it
if we could
SHARE
things:

our favorite books,

our favorite activities,

our favorite treats

(hmmm . . . maybe not the treats).

I hope otters WON'T TEASE me about:

My "Doo-Dee-Doo" song

My extra-large swim fins

My "bad hare days"

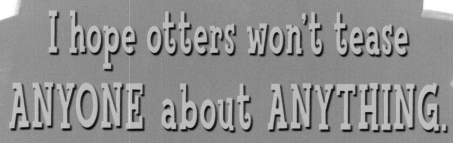

I think otters should **APOLOGIZE** when they do something wrong.

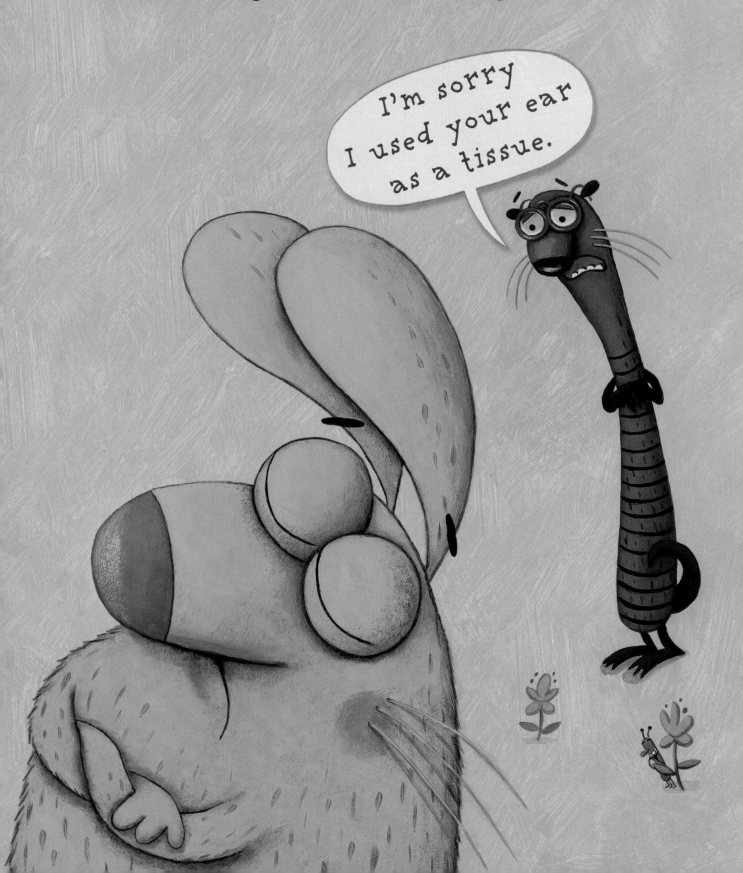

And I hope they can be FORGIVING when I do something wrong.

So there.
That's how I'd
like otters to
treat me.

You see,
Mr. Rabbit,
I told you it
was simple!

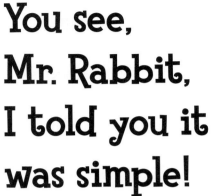

RIGHT! Just "DOO-DEE-DOO unto otters as you would have otters DOO-DEE-DOO unto you!"